Dear mouse friends,
Welcome to the world of

Geronimo Stilton

THE RODENT'S GAZETTE
EDITORIAL STAFF

Geronimo Stilton
A learned and brainy
mouse; editor of
The Rodent's Gazette

Thea Stilton
Geronimo's sister and
special correspondent at
The Rodent's Gazette

Trap Stilton
An awful joker;
Geronimo's cousin and
owner of the store
Cheap Junk for Less

Benjamin Stilton
A sweet and loving
nine-year-old mouse;
Geronimo's favorite
nephew

Geronimo Stilton

MAGICAL MISSION

Scholastic Inc.

If you purchased this book without a cover, you should be aware that this book is stolen property. It was reported as "unsold and destroyed" to the publisher, and neither the author nor the publisher has received any payment for this "stripped book."

Copyright © 2011 by Edizioni Piemme S.p.A., Palazzo Mondadori, Via Mondadori 1, 20090 Segrate, Italy. International Rights © Atlantyca S.p.A. English translation © 2016 by Atlantyca S.p.A.

The publisher does not have any control over and does not assume any responsibility for author or third-party websites or their content.

GERONIMO STILTON names, characters, and related indicia are copyright, trademark, and exclusive license of Atlantyca S.p.A. All rights reserved. The moral right of the author has been asserted. Based on an original idea by Elisabetta Dami. www.geronimostilton.com

Published by Scholastic Inc., *Publishers since 1920*, 557 Broadway, New York, NY 10012. SCHOLASTIC and associated logos are trademarks and/or registered trademarks of Scholastic Inc.

Stilton is the name of a famous English cheese. It is a registered trademark of the Stilton Cheese Makers' Association. For more information, go to www .stiltoncheese.com.

No part of this publication may be reproduced, stored in a retrieval system, or transmitted in any form or by any means, electronic, mechanical, photocopying, recording, or otherwise, without written permission of the copyright holder. For information regarding permission, please contact: Atlantyca S.p.A., Via Leopardi 8, 20123 Milan, Italy; e-mail foreignrights@atlantyca.it, www .atlantyca.com.

This book is a work of fiction. Names, characters, places, and incidents are either the product of the author's imagination or are used fictitiously, and any resemblance to actual persons, living or dead, business establishments, events, or locales is entirely coincidental.

ISBN 978-1-338-03287-1

Text by Geronimo Stilton
Original title *Appuntamento... col mistero!*
Cover by Giuseppe Ferrario (pencils and inks) and Giulia Zaffaroni (color)
Illustrations by Alessandro Muscillo (pencils and inks) and Christian Aliprandi (color)
Graphics by Yuko Egusa and Chiara Cebraro

Special thanks to Kathryn Cristaldi
Translated by Lidia Morson Tramontozzi
Interior design by Kay Petronio

10 9 8 7 6 5 4 3 2 1   16 17 18 19 20

Printed in the U.S.A.   40
First printing 2016

A MYSTERY?
IN LONDON?

One **morning** I was half-listening to the news on TV when a news flash jostled me from my daze.

"Mystery in London's Trafalgar Square!" the announcer squeaked.

I sat up. A *mystery*? In LONDON? Now *that* sounded interesting.

I leaned forward to listen.

"London's **TRAFALGAR SQUARE** is one of the city's most popular tourist destinations. At its center stands Nelson's Column, a monument commemorating Admiral Horatio Nelson, which is guarded by four **immense** bronze lion statues. But recently, one of those lions has been scaring the tails off everyone by **ROARING** insults at passersby! The police at *Scotland Yard* have been unable to explain this disturbing phenomenon . . ."

I turned off the TV and scratched my head.

Hmm . . . A **statue** that roared. Now *there* was a good story for my newspaper!

Oops — I forgot to introduce myself! My name is Stilton, *Geronimo Stilton*. I run *The Rodent's Gazette*, the most famouse newspaper on **MoUse ISLaND**.

Anyway, where was I? Oh yes, I was thinking about the news report. Whoever heard of a talking statue?

Just then I remembered something. The other day I had cut out an interesting article about **London** and **TRAFALGAR SQUARE**. But where had I put it?

I searched the living room, then wandered into my home office. I spotted it immediately, wedged under the corner of

How strange!

my desk — the desk was **wobbly**, and I had used the article to stabilize it!

Pulling out the piece of newspaper, I **smoothed** it and read the paragraph I had remembered: "The renowned art expert Professor Reginald Ratting will be inaugurating the exhibition 'Mice and Cheese in Art' at 11:00 a.m. on Saturday. The exhibit will be on display at the **National Gallery**, one of the leading art museums in London, in Trafalgar Square. Her Majesty the Queen of England will be in attendance."

DON'T HURT ME! TAKE MY CHEESE!

That's it! I knew there was a connection. The main entrance to the National Gallery is on **TRAFALGAR SQUARE** . . . the same square where the **bronze** lion had suddenly started roaring!

Right then I had a terrible thought. What if that lion began **roaring** mean insults during the inauguration? Moldy mozzarella! Poor Professor Ratting would be ḥumiliated right in front of the Queen!

The professor had been my **art history** teacher at college, and I admired him a lot. I felt awful for him.

I paced **BACK** and **fORtH**, thinking

about the talking lion statue. But the more I thought, the less I understood. *What a mystery!*

I'd like to say I spent the rest of the morning trying to figure out the **mystery**, but I didn't. Don't get me wrong, I would have done anything to help *Professor*

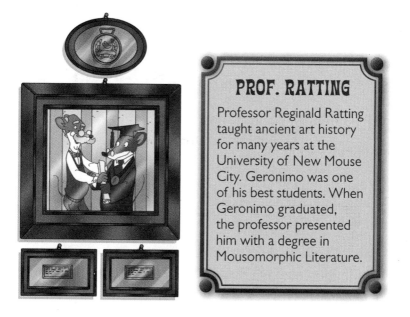

PROF. RATTING

Professor Reginald Ratting taught ancient art history for many years at the University of New Mouse City. Geronimo was one of his best students. When Geronimo graduated, the professor presented him with a degree in Mousomorphic Literature.

Ratting, but I had other things on my mind. Today was the first day of a well-deserved vacation from my hectic office.

I shuffled over to my desk and began surfing the Internet for the perfect place to go on my **VACATION**.

There were so many **OPTIONS**! I could travel to Paris and see the EIFFEL TOWER, or I could go to Athens and take photos of the **Parthenon**, the ancient Greek temple. Then again, if I went to ROME, I could see the famouse *Colosseum*.

What I wanted was a **CULTURAL** vacation. I wanted to learn something exciting, something **INTERESTING**, something new. I surfed for hours, searching for the perfect **vacation** spot until my brain felt like it was about to **EXPLODE**!

Finally, I decided to take a break. I scampered to the cabinet in my living room, hoping for inspiration. Maybe a tasty piece of **vintage** cheese would help.

I was just reaching for a morsel of cheese when out of the corner of my eye, I spotted something flying out of the chimney. It zipped around my head and landed on my snout!

Terrified, I closed my eyes and screeched,

"Don't hurt me! Take my cheese!"

But **nothing** happened. I opened an eye. The thing was still on my snout. I realized I was looking at a **PAPER AIRPLANE**!

How strange! I lifted the plane off my

snout. I **examined** it closely, and saw there was *writing* on the airplane's wing. It **READ**: ......

SUPERSECRET MESSAGE

A **SUPERSECRET** message? Cheese niblets! The only mouse who would send me a supersecret message was my dear friend Kornelius von Kickpaw — Secret Agent 00K! Maybe he needed my help on a **MISSION**. I gulped. Oh no! Whenever I get involved with 00K, I always end up being *SCARED* out of my fur! Plus, I was planning a vacation.

Then I started to feel guilty. Kornelius had been my friend since **ELEMOUSERY SCHOOL**. I thought of all the times he had defended me from the school's bullies. And it was because of him I had become Secret Agent **00G**. (Shhh, don't tell anybody about that! It's a secret!)

RATS! I had no choice. I couldn't turn my back on a friend. I had to help. And so, with my whiskers trembling from fright,

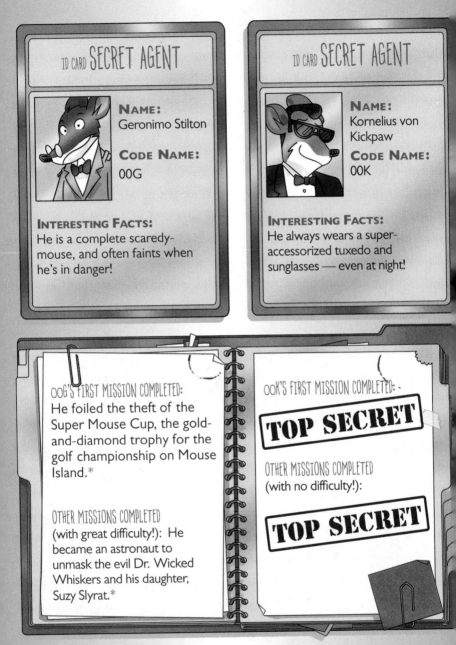

ID CARD SECRET AGENT

NAME:
Geronimo Stilton

CODE NAME:
00G

INTERESTING FACTS:
He is a complete scaredy-mouse, and often faints when he's in danger!

ID CARD SECRET AGENT

NAME:
Kornelius von Kickpaw

CODE NAME:
00K

INTERESTING FACTS:
He always wears a super-accessorized tuxedo and sunglasses — even at night!

00G'S FIRST MISSION COMPLETED:
He foiled the theft of the Super Mouse Cup, the gold-and-diamond trophy for the golf championship on Mouse Island.*

OTHER MISSIONS COMPLETED (with great difficulty!): He became an astronaut to unmask the evil Dr. Wicked Whiskers and his daughter, Suzy Slyrat.*

00K'S FIRST MISSION COMPLETED:

TOP SECRET

OTHER MISSIONS COMPLETED (with no difficulty!):

TOP SECRET

*Read about these adventures in my books *The Giant Diamond Robbery* and *Mouse in Space*!

I slowly opened the little paper plane and read the message . . .

FIRST SUPERSECRET MESSAGE:

Go to the dry cleaner's and pick up my tuxedo right away!

Hmmm . . . what did 00K's **TUX** have to do with anything?

SURPRISE, GERRYKINS!

I read the note over again to be sure I hadn't gotten it wrong.

Nope, the note clearly said, Go to the dry cleaner's and pick up my tuxedo right away!

Well, okay! I **SET** off toward the dry cleaner's. As I walked, I started to feel a GLIMMER of hope. Maybe this **MiSSiON** wouldn't be **dangerous** after all. I had been to the **DRY CLEANER'S** plenty of times. It wasn't the least bit SCARY!

But when I completed that errand and got home, I found another note sticking out of the tux. This one read:

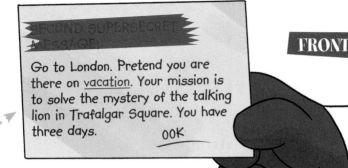

SECOND SUPERSECRET MESSAGE:

Go to London. Pretend you are there on <u>vacation</u>. Your mission is to solve the mystery of the talking lion in Trafalgar Square. You have three days.   00K

FRONT

Great chunks of cheddar! The **ROARING** lion statue in London! Now my whiskers were really trembling. Plus, there was more written on the flip side!

BACK

THIRD SUPERSECRET MESSAGE

Why are you still in New Mouse City, Agent 00G? Get your tail over to London ASAP and solve this mystery!

I threw down the paper and raced to my bedroom. I had to get **packing**!

Oh, if only I were packing for a real

VACATION to London. Instead, I was sneaking off on a secret (and probably TERRIFYING) mission. Gulp!

Then I remembered something that would cheer me up. I hadn't yet finished my TASTY morsel of aged cheese!

I scampered back to my cheese cabinet, drooling in anticipation. But when I opened the door, my jaw hit the ground. The cheese had DISAPPEARED!

Just as I was about to burst into tears, my cousin Trap popped out from behind my living room curtains.

"*SURPRISE, GERRYKINS!*" he squeaked, scampering toward me. "Did you like my little trick?"

I was fuming. "Where's my piece of cheese?" I demanded, *glaring* at Trap.

"Oh, don't be such a **cheesebrain**,

Cuz. Your cheese is still here! It was just a magic trick. I rigged up a bunch of **mirrors** and placed them on a **rotating** base. Then I put the whole thing inside the cabinet and activated it with a remote control."

Trap waved the control in the air. "You see?" he continued. "When I press this **BUttON**, the mirrors reflect the tray with the piece of cheese. When I press the **BUttON** again, one of the mirrors turns, **reflecting** the bottom of the cabinet, so that's all you see. I designed the whole thing myself using my **Magician's Notebook**. Pretty cool, huh?"

Surprise, Gerrykins!

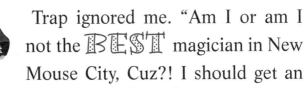

I looked at the notebook, but I couldn't understand a thing! And to be honest, I was too **hungry** to even try.

"Can you please just give me my piece of cheese?" I whined.

Trap ignored me. "Am I or am I not the 𝔹𝔼𝕊𝕋 magician in New Mouse City, Cuz?! I should get an award!" he cried.

Then, before I could squeak, he grabbed my ℙ𝕣𝕖𝕔𝕚𝕠𝕦𝕤 piece of aged cheese and popped it into his mouth! A **SMILE** spread across his snout. "Very tasty!" he pronounced.

I was **FURIOUS**! "That's it, Trap! I don't have time for your tricks! I'm leaving on a mission — I mean, a 𝕋ℝ𝕀ℙ. I've got to get ready," I *squeaked* angrily.

"Really? What a coincidence. I'm getting ready to leave, too. Where are you headed?"

Obviously I couldn't tell Trap the details of my **SECRET MISSION** (otherwise, it wouldn't be a secret!), so I told him I was going on vacation. "They're opening an art exhibit on **MICE AND CHEESE IN ART** at the National Gallery in London," I said.

MAGICAL ILLUSION

Magical illusion is a form of entertainment where the illusionist — the performer, often called a magician — uses special effects that make the impossible seem possible. Magicians use tricks and props that may be mechanical, chemical, hydraulic, optical, or psychological.

Trap yawned. "An art exhibit? Can you say 'BORING'?!" he scoffed. "But as it turns out, I'm going to London, too! I'll be there for a much more exciting event, though. I'm going to compete in — and, of course, win! — the Ultimate Trick. It's a competition to determine the world's greatest MAGICIAN!"

TAKE ONLY A TINY SUITCASE!

Trap scurried past me to my computer and began typing **FURIOUSLY**. I peered over his shoulder in a panic. What was my annoying cousin up to now?

"All done!" Trap shouted before I could ask. "I just booked us **first-class** plane tickets, since you're paying; five-star **luxury** hotel rooms, since you're paying; and I made reservations at five **EXCLUSIVE** restaurants, since you're paying. Aren't you **LUCKY** we're traveling together?"

I chewed my whiskers to keep from **SCREAMING**. There was no way I wanted to travel with Trap.

Suddenly, I thought of something. If Trap and I traveled together, I would be less noticeable. The **Ultimate Trick** competition could be my cover!

Forcing a smile, I squeaked, "Sounds **PERFECT**, Trap!"

Uh-oh!

Booked it!

"Enough jabbering, Gerrykins. You better get packing — we've gotta make our flight. And take only a TiNY SUiTCASe, got it?"

I didn't understand why, but I hurried to pack a tiny suitcase with just the bare minimum.

Then we called a taxi and stopped by Trap's house to pick up his luggage. When I saw his bag, I understood why he insisted that I travel LIGHT. His **giant suitcase** was as big and as **HEAVY** as a refrigerator!

At the airport, Trap made me **haul** my tiny suitcase *and* his giant suitcase.

"I'm a *BRILLIANT* magician!" he boasted. "You don't want me to get tired, do you?"

Already I was regretting my decision to travel with my cousin, but what could I do?

With a groan, I **DRAGGED** the two suitcases through the airport to the baggage check. (Cheese and crackers, that giant suitcase was **heavy**!)

The security guard jumped back in surprise when Trap opened his luggage for inspection.

Boing! Flap! Pop!

Hurry up, Cuz!

Pant!

The suitcase was jam-packed with **MAGIC TRICKS**. There were double-bottomed containers, inflatable doves, fake rabbits, **multicolored** handkerchiefs, **DISAPPEARING** playing cards, and lots of other peculiar objects. It took forever for Trap to get everything back into the suitcase! How **embarrassing**!

By the time we boarded our flight to London, I was ready for a **LOOOONG** nap. Unfortunately, as soon as we sat down, Trap declared, "You're in for a treat, Cuz! I'm going to give you a taste of my amazing **MAGICAL** talents! Get ready to witness the **WORLD'S GREATEST MAGICIAN**!"

Without another word, he **JUMPED** into the middle of the aisle. "Hello, everyone! My name is Trap and I am on my way to compete in — and win! — the ultimate Trick, the greatest competition of illusionists in the world. And now I would like to **perform** for you one of my **ASTOUNDING**, amazing, unbelievable magic tricks!"

I sank **LOW** into my seat, hoping no one would notice me. At that moment, Trap announced, "My cousin Geronimo will be my assistant! He's a bit of a **cheesebrain**, but he's the best I can do!"

First, Trap asked the passengers for some coins. He put them in a container, and then made them **disappear**. Everyone applauded.

So far, so good. Too bad Trap couldn't figure out how to make the **MONEY** reappear! Pretty soon the passengers **STOPPED** applauding and started to boo!

"**Don't worry**," said Trap. "The show isn't over. Now my assistant will find your coins! Hurry up, Geronimo. Don't keep the nice rodents waiting."

And that's how I ended up looking like a cheesebrain. I **LOOKED** and **LOOKED**, but those coins seemed to have **DISAPPEARED** into thin air!

The passengers were **FURIOUS**. Just when I thought things were about to get **ugly**, Trap stuck his paw in my **POCKET** . . . and pulled out the coins!

Everyone **APPLAUDED**. "That magician is great, but his assistant, Geronimo Stilton, is a real **cheesebrain**," they remarked.

I'm so Hungry, I Could Eat Big Ben!

After the plane landed, we took a taxi to **LONDON**. We got to the city just in time for breakfast.

"I'm starving," Trap moaned. "I'm so hungry, I could eat **ten** cheese donuts. No, make that two **cheddar subs**. No, wait, I've got it — I'm so hungry, I could eat **Big Ben**!*"

I was pretty hungry, too. My stomach growled loudly:

GROOOARRR!

Right then, Trap grabbed my paw. "Hey, let's take a **BOAT** ride down the Thames. Check it out!"

*Big Ben is the nickname of a large bell in the iconic clock tower of the Houses of Parliament in London. The name can also refer to the tower itself.

I looked at the pier where my cousin was pointing and saw a sign next to the most *luxurious* yacht:

THE ROYAL SQUEAKER

SUPER-MEGA-LUXURY TOUR
(English breakfast included)

There was something written in tiny letters at the bottom of the sign. I tried to read it but didn't have time before Trap yanked me down the **gangplank**. I struggled onto the boat with the suitcases.

The view of the **CITY** from the boat was breathtaking. I was just beginning to relax and enjoy it when four waiters dressed in black tuxedos SCURRIED

London Eye
(a giant Ferris wheel)

THE THAMES

The Thames is the river that runs through London and connects to the sea. Centuries ago, this river made it possible for London to develop its commercial strength and its naval empire. Some of the creatures that live in the Thames include otters and eels.

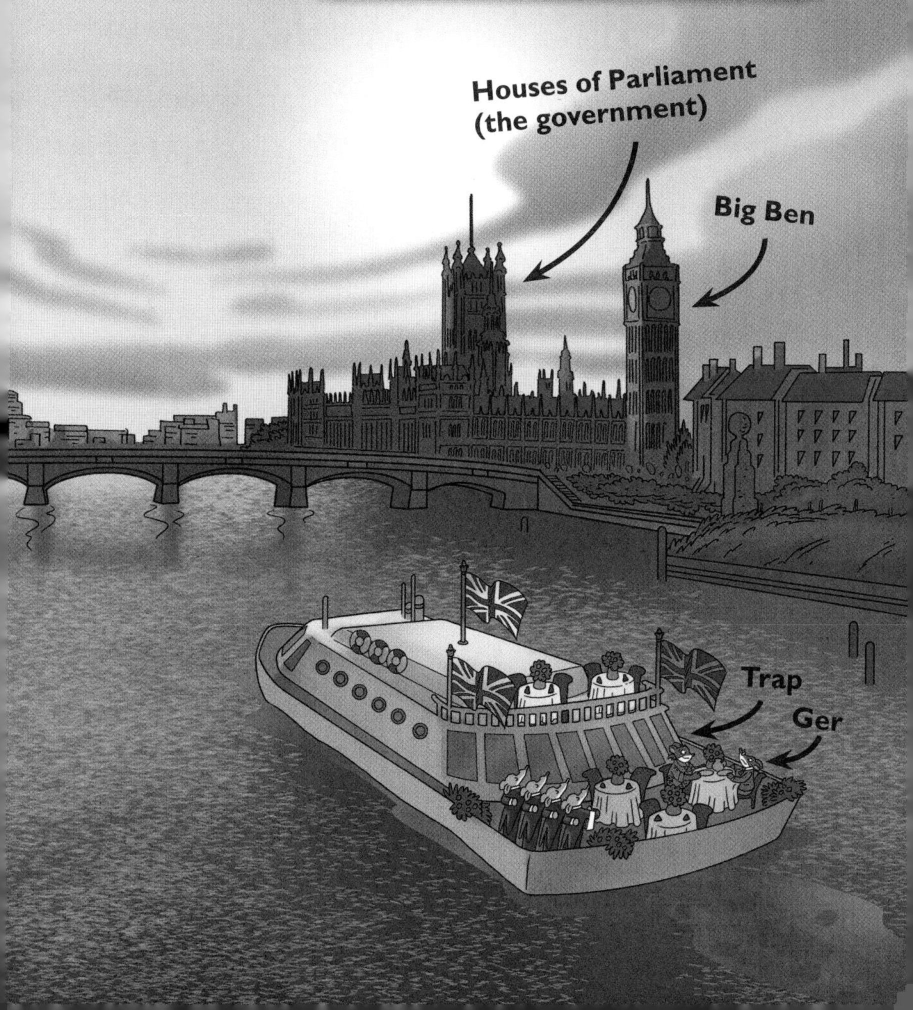

Houses of Parliament
(the government)

Big Ben

Trap

Ger

up to us. They bowed so low their whiskers **BRUSHED** the floor.

"Welcome, guests!" one of them said in a *formal* voice. "Gentlemice, follow me, if you please! Breakfast will be served immediately." He backed away with another bow.

We sat down at a table beautifully set for two. It was covered with an EXPENSIVE paw-embroidered linen tablecloth, and the chairs were **soft** velvet. An arrangement of extremely rare **purple** orchids was placed in the center of the table.

Our plates were made of fine china. And the name of the yacht, ***The Royal Squeaker***, was engraved on each piece of silverware.

How stylish!
How classy!
How luxurious!

The waiters were very attentive. They announced each dish of **FOOD** as they served us. Each platter was overflowing. I guess the English truly believe that **breakfast** is the most important meal of the day — I had never been served **so much** for breakfast in my life!

We ate bacon and eggs, sausage, grilled tomatoes, grilled mushrooms, beans in tomato sauce, and hot **blueberry** muffins and scones.

To drink we had a STEAMING pot of tea and fresh-squeezed orange juice.

I tried not to eat too much, but everything was so delicious. I couldn't stop myself! In the end I was **stuffed** up to my eyeballs!

"Yum, yum, yum! I love London!" Trap shouted, shoveling down his food.

Finally, he massaged his tummy and let out a loud **BUUURP**!

The waiters shook their heads in disapproval.

Oh, my cousin was so **embarrassing**!

Piping-hot tea

Muffins, scones, and jam

Bacon, sausage, tomatoes, and mushrooms

After that, the waiters brought us each a chewable tablet for indigestion on a **SILVER TRAY**. The bill was brought on another silver tray — along with a bottle of *cheese-scented smelling salts*! That's exactly what I needed, because when I read the bill I almost **fainted**. It was so expensive!

Hard-boiled eggs, scrambled eggs, eggs over easy . . .

What a meal!

Yeah!

Mega-antacid

I had to use **three** different credit cards to cover the bill (one wouldn't do it!). When I handed them to the waiter I said, "I had no idea your cruise was so expensive."

Super-expensive bill!

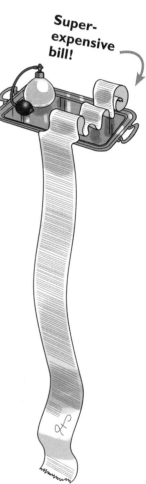

"Didn't you read the smaII print on our sign?" The head waiter sniffed. He got the sign out and showed me. This time, I read the tiny print.

It said, *This is the* ROYAL SQUEAKER TOUR. *If your pockets are not as* **deep** *as the* *royals', do not bother boarding!*

Holey cheese! I felt like a *royal* fool!

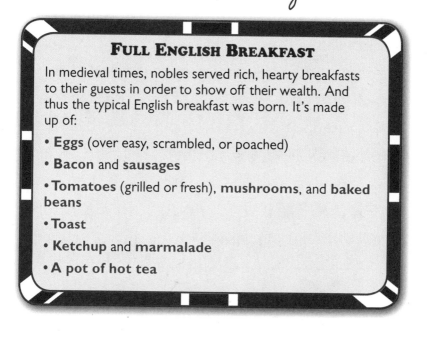

FULL ENGLISH BREAKFAST

In medieval times, nobles served rich, hearty breakfasts to their guests in order to show off their wealth. And thus the typical English breakfast was born. It's made up of:

• **Eggs** (over easy, scrambled, or poached)

• **Bacon** and **sausages**

• **Tomatoes** (grilled or fresh), **mushrooms**, and **baked beans**

• **Toast**

• **Ketchup** and **marmalade**

• **A pot of hot tea**

SHOO! SHOO!

Eventually, we arrived back at the pier and disembarked. I dragged our suitcases down the gangplank with a *sinking* feeling. My stomach was **FULL**, but my wallet was practically **EMPTY**! Rats!

I trudged along the streets of London **GRUMBLING** to myself, "So much for my vacation. I'll be broke before we even hit the hotel!"

As I lumbered along, a pigeon landed on my head and began pecking me.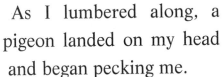

"Shoo! Shoo! Go away!" I squeaked. It didn't take the hint. Instead, it deposited a nice little **present** on my ear! **Yuck!**

While I was cleaning myself off, I noticed a little **NOTE** tied to the pigeon's foot. Curious, I unrolled it. It was a **SUPERSECRET** message!

00G, move your paws! You are not on vacation — you are on a mission! Stop stuffing your snout and making a scene with those ridiculous suitcases!

Well, what are you waiting for? Get going!   00K

Holey cheese! I felt terrible! 00K was right. I hadn't done ONe WHiSKeR of research for my mission. I had to get cracking and figure out what was making that lion **ROAR**.

I **scurried** to catch up to Trap, who

was way ahead of me (since I was dragging his super-stuffed GIGANTIC suitcase!). *Whistling* a cheerful tune, he was happily taking in the sights of the city.

I was about to suggest we head over to **Trafalgar Square** so I could begin my research when Trap let out a shriek. "We better get going, Cuz! The changing of the guard at *Buckingham Palace* is taking place in a few minutes! We can't miss it! It's a **MUST-SEE** for every London tourist!"

Before I could protest, he pulled me onto a DOUBLE-DECKER bus. I wanted to stay down below but Trap insisted we ride on the upper level. Within a few minutes I began feeling sick . . . **very**, **very**, **very** sick!

Here are two things you should know

about me: **1** I am afraid of **HEIGHTS**, and **2** I am prone to motion sickness!

Luckily, before I totally lost my breakfast, the bus pulled up in front of *Buckingham Palace.*

Double-decker bus

Gulp!

BUCKINGHAM PALACE

This beautiful palace is the London residence of the reigning monarch. It has 775 rooms total. When the Royal Standard (the official flag of the British monarch) is up, it means the sovereign is home. Otherwise, the Union Flag flies. The changing of the guard ceremony takes place in front of the palace!

They're amazing!

We stood in front of the palace gate and were quickly SURROUNDED by a crowd of tourists. The Queen's Guard paraded in the square in full uniform, which included distinctive **red** jackets and **BLACK** hats. Part of the guard were a band, and played iṅstrumėṅts as they marched.

HOW EXCITING!

Suddenly, one of the clarinet players took a slightly **SHORT** step just as the trombone player behind him extended his **LONG** slide. The slide hit the clarinet player's tall 𝕗𝕦𝕣𝕣𝕪 black hat, and it flew up into the air. Moldy mozzarella! It was headed straight toward me!

Hey, look! He lost his hat!

Uh-oh!

Boing!

To my horror, it landed with a **THUD** on my head and slid down over my eyes. Ack! I couldn't see a thing! Before I could pull the hat off, a **POLICEMOUSE** squeaked, "Hey, what are you two doing with the **ROYAL GUARD'S HAT**?"

"Don't look at me. It's all my cousin's fault!" Trap answered.

I turned **red** from the tip of my tail to the end of my whiskers. **How embarrassing!** I tried to explain that it wasn't my fault. I would never **steal** anything, especially a hat. I didn't even look good in hats! But the policemouse didn't **believe** me!

He took out a book of tickets and began

scribbling away, muttering under his breath, "Let's see, here's a **ticket** for possession of non-authorized royal headgear, a ticket for having lied to a policemouse, a ticket for arguing with a policemouse . . ."

Tsk, tsk, tsk, Gerrykins . . .

GET OUT OF THE
WAY, CHEESEBRAIN!

By the time the policemouse was finished, I had about **FIVE HUNDRED** tickets in my paws! Well, okay, maybe not actually **FIVE HUNDRED**, but you get the picture. Oh, how do I get myself into these ridiculous situations?!

"Now stay out of **TROUBLE**!" the policemouse warned.

"Don't worry, sir, I'll keep an eye on him!" Trap said as I turned three shades **redder**.

Finally, we got directions to **Trafalgar Square** and headed off toward it.

At the center of the square, overlooking two **HUGE** fountains, stood a **tall** column

TRAFALGAR SQUARE

This square derives its name from the naval battle of Cape Trafalgar in 1805. Admiral Horatio Nelson, who led the English fleet to victory but died in the battle, is immortalized by the statue that stands at the center of the square. The square is used for many different types of community gatherings and demonstrations, including a large New Year's Eve celebration!

Here we are!

with a statue of Admiral Nelson on top. Four enormouse bronze **LION** statues reclined at its base.

I was ecstatic. Finally, I could start working on my **SECRET MISSION**! As 00K had suggested, I acted as though I were a tourist on vacation, but really began looking for **clues**. I walked around the column, inspecting each of the four lions carefully. One of them was the **talking** lion. Which one?

I didn't have to wait long to find out. Just as Trap and I were approaching one lion, it roared, "Get out of the way, Cheesebrain!"

I was so shocked, I nearly *JUMPED* out of my fur!

My cousin, on the other paw, was furious. He **MARCHED** up to the lion, demanding,

"Hey, do you know who you are insulting?! I'm Trap Stilton, and I'm going to win the **Ultimate Trick** and be crowned the world's greatest magician!"

I tried to make him keep **QUIET** because I noticed that the policemouse from earlier had followed us. The last thing I needed was a **TICKET** for disturbing public lion statues!

How dare you?!

Get down this instant!

"Lion or no lion, he can't call me a cheesebrain!" Trap snorted. Then he rubbed his belly. "All of this excitement has gotten me **hungry**. How about a snack?" he suggested.

I was still stuffed from the big breakfast we had eaten on the *Royal Squeaker*. Plus, I wanted to concentrate on my secret mission. So I promised Trap I'd meet him at the theater, in time for the start of the **Ultimate Trick**.

As soon as my cousin left, I bought a newspaper to hide behind. Then I stood by the statue with my snout in the pages, waiting for the lion to talk again. I waited for **HOURS** and **HOURS** but the lion didn't say one word.

While I waited, questions about the lion **RACED** through my brain. **WHY** had the lion talked before? **WHY** was it now keeping quiet? **WHY** was the lion always **INSULTING** everyone instead of saying anything nice? Someone needed to teach that lion some **manners**!

I know it sounds **crazy**, but before I knew it, I started lecturing the lion. "You know, lion," I began, **staring** into the statue's eyes. "It's not nice to pick on vISitoRS, and —"

I was interrupted by someone **coughing** behind me. I turned and saw a rodent with a thick *mustache*.

"Mr. Stilton, do you remember me? I'm *Professor Ratting*," he said.

I was so embarrassed. My old professor had just caught me talking to a **BRONZE STATUE**!

"Of course, Professor," I replied, shaking his paw.

Next to the professor stood a very well-dressed lady. "This is my wife, Lady Ratting, Senior Lady-in-Waiting to the Queen," said the professor.

Now I was **doubly** embarrassed! Lucky for me, the Rattings seemed to be okay with me SQUeAKiNg with a statue. The next thing I knew, they invited me back to their mansion for high tea. We had gourmet cheese tarts and delicious tea! **Yum!**

After I had eaten the last tart, the professor leaned in close and said, "Mr. Stilton, we know that you are not only a writer, but also a **SECRET AGENT**. Now I'm going to tell you a secret. I'm a friend of Agent

Thank you!

OOK, and . . . I'm also a secret agent! Just call me **OOR**!"

I grinned. I was glad I wasn't the only **SECRET AGENT** in the room. It's nice to have someone on your side.

"I haven't been able to **crack** this case, which is why OOK sent you to help me," he continued. Then he handed me a sheet of paper. "Read what this terrible crook wants."

RANCID RICOTTA! It was a very **THREATENING** note!

Didn't you love the lion statue roaring insults? No? **WELL, IT'S ONLY THE BEGINNING!**

Hand over the **CROWN JEWELS** or there'll be even worse pranks coming your way soon!

Deliver the jewels tonight, **BY MIDNIGHT**, inside a big suitcase. Leave them in front of the talking lion!

Lady Ratting shivered. "Oh, Mr. Stilton, I'm so worried," she cried.

I wasn't worried. I was PETRIFIED! Still, I couldn't let the Rattings know I was a scaredy-mouse. So I took a deep breath and said, "Don't worry, I'll catch the crook before midnight!"

Now if only I had a clue how to do that!

THE ULTIMATE TRICK!

By the time I left the Rattings' house it was evening, and I had to SCURRY to the theater. I spotted Trap in his **magician's** outfit and scampered over to sit next to him.

The master of ceremonies onstage began squeaking. "Welcome to the Ultimate Trick, the greatest competition of illusionists in the world! Before the show begins, I will read aloud the RULES by which each contestant must abide. After that, we will begin the show. May the best mouse win!"

While we were listening to the rules, Trap pointed out some of the FAMOUSE MAGICIANS in the crowd.

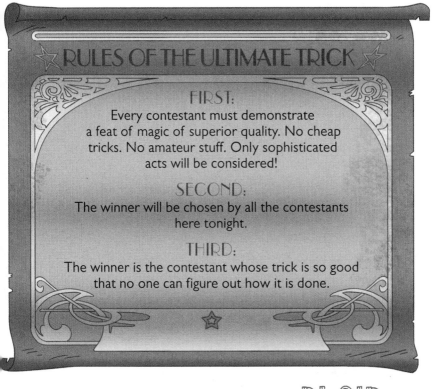

RULES OF THE ULTIMATE TRICK

FIRST:
Every contestant must demonstrate a feat of magic of superior quality. No cheap tricks. No amateur stuff. Only sophisticated acts will be considered!

SECOND:
The winner will be chosen by all the contestants here tonight.

THIRD:
The winner is the contestant whose trick is so good that no one can figure out how it is done.

"See the mouse dressed in the PLAID KILT? That's Liam McCheesy from Scotland. The rodent next to him with the RED suspenders is Franz von Furmeister of Germany."

I nodded, trying to look interested.

"The one with the matador's hat is José Spicysnout from Spain. He's super popular with the lady mice. And Jean Paul Le Paws of France, the one with the **tOP Hat**, is supposed to have an unbelievable show. Then there's that magician in the last row with the **CHeDDaR-COLOReD** cape. He calls himself **Mystery Mouse**, and that is the perfect name for him. No one knows **ANYTHING** about him!"

By then, I have to admit, my mind had started to **wander**. Instead of listening to my cousin, I was thinking about the *promise* I had made to Professor Ratting. How could I help him solve the case?

My thoughts were interrupted by the first contestant on stage. *Franz von Fuhmeister* reached into his hat and squeaked, "Let me introduce you to Hopper, my **rabbit**. He's right here in my hat!"

But no rabbit appeared.

"Hopper can be *shy*," von Furmeister muttered. He looked around the stage. "Hopper, come out right now! Stop EMBARRASSING me!"

And that's when I felt something inside my jacket.

"Ha, ha! You're tickling me!" I squeaked. It was the rabbit!

Everybody turned to look at me. Now I

There it is!

was totally embarrassed. "Um, sorry, I just **HOPPED**, I mean, Hopper, the rabbit, **HOPPED**, not me! I mean, I know how to hop, but I didn't . . ." I babbled. The crowd kept staring. Too bad I wasn't a magician — if I were, I would have made myself DISAPPEAR!

Meanwhile, the rabbit took off down the aisle and von Furmeister *raced* after him.

"He didn't train his rabbit well," Trap observed.

"Disqualified!" the crowd squeaked in agreement.

Liam McCheesy was up next. Luckily, he didn't have a rabbit. Instead, he brought out a painting of a FLOWERING meadow.

"Look closely," he instructed. Then he began to count, "One, two . . ."

On three, he touched the painting, and a **dove** flew across it. Trap snorted. "That's not a painting!" he exclaimed. "It's a **flat-screen TV**!"

He ran backstage and **unplugged** an electrical cord attached to the painting. The painting went dark. The magician turned red.

"Liam McCheesy is **disqualified**!" everyone shouted.

The contest continued, but one after another, each magician was disqualified. Finally, the host announced, "All right, everyone. Don't give up hope. We'll find the **Ultimate Trick.** Now please put your paws together for our next contestant, Mystery Mouse, and his talking vest!"

A rodent wearing a velvet **CHEDDAR-COLORED** cape walked on stage. His mouth was closed, but a spooky voice said, "Good evening!"

We all looked around but couldn't figure out who had spoken. **MYSTERY MOUSE** smiled.

"Say hello to my **talking vest!**" he squeaked.

He opened his cape, and a huge **CLOWN** mouth appeared on his vest.

"Everyone clap your paws!" the vest said in an eerie voice. "Let's hear it for **MYSTERY MOUSE**, the greatest magician in the world!"

"Oooooooooooohhhhh!"

the crowd squeaked in appreciation.

As everyone applauded, I heard my cousin snorting.

"Is it another flat-screen TV?" I asked.

Trap shook his head. "Nope," he said. "It's a **PROJECTOR**!" He sprinted to the opposite end of the theater and located the projector. Then he put his face in front of it, and his SILHOUETTE appeared on the vest!

"This is how the **TRICK** is done!" my cousin declared. "He's using a projector!"

He ran on the stage and pulled out a tiny speaker attached to Mystery Mouse's vest. "This is where the **voice** comes from!" Trap said, raising it triumphantly. "It was taped!"

"Mystery Mouse is disqualified!" the crowd shouted.

I'll be back!

Trap returned to his seat looking smug.

Meanwhile, **MYSTERY MOUSE** stormed off the stage, shaking a paw at my cousin. "How dare you laugh at me!" he thundered. "I'm leaving . . . but not for good! You'll be hearing from Mystery Mouse, and that's a promise!"

Thinking about that talking vest gave me an idea related to the **talking lion**!

Quietly, I snuck out of the auditorium and back to Trap's dressing room. His **ENORMOUSE** suitcase lay empty on the floor. Trap must have needed everything for his performance. Perfect! I borrowed it. That **SUITCASE** was just what I needed to convince the mysterious crook who had written that note that I was cooperating. I would deliver it to the square by midnight.

I started dragging the suitcase down the hall when I passed by the costume closet. I spotted a box filled with **FAKE JEWELRY**. Perfect! I borrowed it. It would look like the crown jewels. **Huffing** and **puffing**, I left the theater. Pulling that huge suitcase was making me hugely exhausted!

I Did It! I Did It!

It was dark when I arrived at **Trafalgar Square**. It was almost midnight, and I was running out of time. I had to **HURRY** and solve the case!

I left the suitcase next to the talking lion and began looking for clues. Too bad I had no idea what I was looking for! I was starting to panic when I noticed something strange on the ground by the lion. It was a dark, **RAISED** object that looked like an upside-down bowl. I stepped on it.

"Get out of the way, Cheesebrain!" roared the lion.

"Slimy Swiss cheese! This device makes the lion talk!" I exclaimed happily. I had a feeling that the talking lion was actually an illusion just like Mystery Mouse's TRICK at the competition — created by a projected image and a speaker.

So if my suspicions were correct, I'd find a hidden **projector** somewhere, projecting the image of a moving mouth onto the STATUE'S face, creating the illusion that it was talking. And if I was correct again, I'd also find a **hidden** speaker emitting the lion's voice!

Get out of the way, Cheesebrain!

Secret button to make the lion talk

By now, my whiskers were trembling with fear. But I had to find out the truth! With my heart pounding, I climbed onto the statue. To my relief, I found a tiny speaker inside the lion's MOUTH! Now the only thing to find was the projector.

I looked carefully around the square and noticed that one of the dolphins in the fountain opposite the statue wasn't SPURTING any water. Could it be?

I hated to ruin my good suit, but I had no choice. I scampered to the fountain and dove in.

SPLASH!

I swam over to the dolphin statue and found exactly what I was looking for. A tiny projector was fastened to the dolphin's head! And it was projecting an IMAGE of the lion moving its mouth!

I was so excited, I began splashing and singing at the top of my lungs.

I did it! I did it!

I solved the mystery! Not Scotland Yard or the Queen herself! Just me, me, me, me, me!"

That's when I heard a gruff voice behind me say, "You again?"

I turned and saw the same POLICEMOUSE

Projector

Can't you see the projector?!

Excuses, excuses!

who had given me a pawful of tickets at Buckingham Palace! He shook his snout and began writing me more **TICKETS**.

"A **TICKET** for disturbing the public peace. A **TICKET** for swimming in the fountain. A **TICKET** for climbing on the dolphin . . ."

I tried to explain, but the policemouse wouldn't listen. He handed me the tickets and **marched** off into the night.

Rancid rat hairs! This case was costing me a **fortune**! I had to catch the crook before I went totally broke!

I got to work putting my plan in action.

1 First I **PAINTED** the suitcase's handle with a special **FLUORESCENT** paint. (Trap uses it in his ghost act.)

2 Then I tied a transparent string to the **handle** of the suitcase. (Trap uses it for his Moving Mouseball trick.)

3 Then I dumped a bottle of skunk stink all over the suitcase. (Trap uses it in his Stink Bomb act.)

4 Then I sprinkled **itching powder** over everything. (Trap uses it to play pranks on me!)

Finally, I hid behind the fountain and waited . . .

At the stroke of midnight, a rodent **scurried** furtively across the square and headed for the suitcase. He was wrapped in a cape the color of **cheddar cheese**. (I thought I had seen that cape before . . . but I was so afraid of the mysterious rodent, I couldn't think straight.)

My heart was POUNDING out of my fur as I watched the crook opening the suitcase. He rummaged through the contents and **THUNDERED**, "These aren't the crown jewels. They're fakes!"

Then he **SCREECHED**, "What a **stench**!" Then he began scratching himself like a crazed rat. I quickly pulled the string.

The lid of the giant suitcase **SLAMMED** shut on the crook's paw!

I sprinted toward him shouting, "**Stop! Thief!**"

Still **scratching**, he ran off in a cloud of stench. I tried to catch him, but I **slipped** on the wet pavement, flew into the air, and landed on my tail. Oof!

DISQUALIFIED!

I dragged my aching tail back to the theater, feeling like a **furry** failure. How had I let that crook slip through my paws? What would I tell *Professor Ratting*? What would I tell **OOK**? Would my tail ever stop throbbing?

I arrived at the theater just in time for Trap's act: the **Moving Mouseball**.

Trap pointed to a crystal ball lying on a table. A spotlight cast the **SHADOW** of his finger on the curtain behind him, and another spotlight cast the **SHADOW** of the ball.

"Watch as I move the mouseball with my **magic** shadow finger," Trap instructed.

Everyone watched.

"I'll remain here, far from the table. As you can see, it is impossible for my paw to reach the ball," my cousin continued. "Now look at the SHADOWS on the wall behind me. The ball and I are far from each other, but my paw's shadow is very NEAR the ball's shadow."

The crowd nodded.

"Keep watching," Trap went on.

Everyone sat up for a **CLOSER** look. Trap pointed his finger forward. His finger's shadow touched the shadow of the ball . . . and the **actual ball** fell off the table and rolled on the floor! **Incredible!**

Everyone **APPLAUDED**. All except Mystery Mouse, the magician with the **talking** vest. He leaped onto the stage.

"Mr. Stilton, you exposed my trick. Now I'll expose yours!" he sneered.

I noticed that he was furiously **scratching** his ear. **STRANGE!**

Mystery Mouse continued explaining. "Any amateur can perform that trick. All you need is a piece of tape and some transparent string! You tape one end of the string to the ball and hold the other end."

As Mystery Mouse was talking, I noticed a terrible **stench** was filling the theater. It seemed to be coming from the magician. Flies *buzzed* around his cape. **STRANGE!**

Meanwhile, Mystery Mouse was holding up the ball and attached string. "Ta-da! Here's your Moving Mouseball," he said to the crowd.

"**DISQUALIFIED!**" everyone shouted.

What a stench!

Transparent string!

At this point, the master of ceremonies appeared on stage. "Well, folks, I'm afraid this year we do not have a winner in the Ultimate Trick competition. But thanks, everyone, for coming out!"

My cousin looked like he was about to EXPLODE. If there is one thing you should know about Trap, it's that he hates to LOSE!

"Just a minute!" he squeaked. "Who says the *Stilton family* won't win?! You haven't seen my cousin's number yet! Tomorrow, my astonishing cousin Geronimo will perform an astounding feat of magic. He will make Big Ben disappear! Not to brag, but it's a little trick I taught him!"

Everyone in the theater fell SILENT. They looked at me openmouthed. Then everyone gathered around me, asking a million questions.

"Is it true that **Trap** taught you everything? Do you know how much Big Ben weighs? Do you think you can **LiFT** it by yourself?"

I tried protesting, but Trap had already assembled a **PRESS CONFERENCE**. Of course, he told the crowd that he was the one who had taught me everything. I rolled my eyes. But I was actually quite nervous — how in the world was I supposed to make Big Ben disappear?!

Feeling like a complete fraud, I shut myself in my hotel room and tried to think of a way to make BIG BEN vanish.

This was crazy! I was a newspapermouse, not a magician. Headlines flashed before my eyes: *Stilton's Big Flop at Big Ben! Disappearing Act Disappoints!*

I tried to concentrate on BIG BEN,

but I had too much on my mind. After all, the whole reason I had traveled to London was to solve the mystery of the **TALKING** lion. Becoming the world's greatest **MAGICIAN** was never part of my plan.

Still, the more I thought about the magic competition and the mystery of the talking lion, the more confused I became. There was something strange about that Mystery Mouse that I just couldn't put my paw on. Why was he **scratching**? And why was he so **stinky**? Could he possibly be the mysterious rodent I had seen at **Trafalgar Square**? I needed more **PROOF**.

I'M IN BIG TROUBLE!

I decided there was only one thing to do: get **HELP** fast! So I picked up the phone and called one of the **bravest** mice I know . . . my sister!

"Hi, Thea? It's Geronimo. I'm in **BIG TROUBLE**!" I squeaked as soon as she answered.

"How big?" asked Thea.

"As big as BIG BEN! Trap promised everybody in London that tomorrow I'd make it **DISAPPEAR**! What should I do?!"

"**HOLEY CHEESE!**" Thea exclaimed. "You *are* in trouble!"

I explained about Trap and the Ultimate Trick competition. "Somehow, he thinks I can **WIN** the competition for him!" I squeaked, twisting my tail up in a knot.

"It's okay, Ger," Thea said. "I'll take the next flight out. Don't worry. I just thought of a **FABUMOUSE iDEA**!"

I said good-bye and hung up the phone. I didn't know what she had in mind, but if my sister said she had an idea, I had nothing to worry about. **Thea** always knows how to get out of a jam. You can bet your WHiSKeRS on it!

I let out a long sigh of relief. Now that Thea was working on the magic trick, I could finally concentrate on solving the **mystery** of the talking lion.

Although it was late, I called Professor Ratting to give him an update.

"Professor Ratting? It's Geronimo. I figured out how the lion talks!" I announced. Then I explained about the PROJECTOR I had found on the dolphin fountain at Trafalgar Square. "Meet me tomorrow in front of Big Ben. I'll be performing a little magic trick. I'm hoping to rat out the mysterious crook during the show," I added.

"I didn't know you did magic tricks," the professor commented.

"Um, well, it's no BIG deal," I stammered. If only the professor knew my little trick involved BIG BEN!

The following morning, I scurried to the square directly across the Thames from BIG BEN. That was where I would perform my magic trick. I was a nervous wreck. Everyone was counting on me!

When I got there, I saw some **familiar** faces. My sister, Thea, was there, along with my nephew Benjamin and his friend Bugsy Wugsy!

"Am I glad to see you!" I squeaked, giving each mouse a **HUGE HUG**.

"Don't **worry**, Gerrykins. I've got everything under control," said Thea. "Check out the stage we set up for your act." It was

Look!

a big **round** platform that had lots of seats for the audience, a small stage up front, and huge *red velvet* curtains surrounding it.

"What do you think, Uncle Geronimo?" asked Benjamin.

Before I could answer, a **crowd** of spectators began filing into the seats. *I think I'm about to faint!* I thought.

Thea marched up to the **stage**, pulling me along behind her. "Good morning, everyone!" she began. "I'm the **ASSISTANT** to the great magician Geronimo Stilton. Please take a seat so we can start the show!"

My heart began pounding under my fur. Moldy mozzarella! I was about to become the **LAUGHINGSTOCK** of London! But before I could slink away in total humiliation, Thea placed a *golden rope* hanging from the curtain in my paw.

"Relax," she whispered to me. "All you have to do is pull this rope **T** **H** **R** **E** **E** times. The curtains will open and close. I'll take care of the rest!"

She turned to the audience and squeaked, "And now the great Geronimo will make Big Ben disappear!"

I pulled the rope once. The curtains opened, but BIG BEN was still there!

MYSTERY MOUSE'S SECRET

Red with **embarrassment**, I closed the curtains and stammered, "Heh, heh, I'll try again . . . Let me just pull this rope, and . . ."

I pulled the *rope* again. When the curtains opened, Big Ben was . . . still there!

"**BOOOOOOO!**" the crowd heckled. I hurriedly closed the curtains again.

As I stared out into the audience, I noticed a rodent with flies **BUZZING** around him. It was Mystery Mouse! He was **SCRATCHING** like crazy. I just knew he was responsible for the talking lion. But how could I prove it?

Meanwhile, the **crowd** was getting restless.

"Get off the stage! You stink!" they cried.

I had to make the tower disappear, and pronto! With whiskers T̶R̶E̶M̶B̶L̶I̶N̶G̶, I closed my eyes and pulled the rope for the third time. This time I was ready for boos and for **ROTTEN FOOD** to be thrown at me. Instead, everything became very quiet. I opened my eyes. The audience was gaping in surprise.

The tower had disappeared!

The stage curtains framed an empty blue sky!

The audience erupted in shouts of surprise.

"IT'S GONE!"

The master of ceremonies shook my **paw** and declared, "Geronimo Stilton is the **WINNER**

of the Ultimate Trick!"

"I knew you could do it!" squeaked Trap. "After all, I **TAUGHT** you everything you know!"

"You're in big **TROUBLE** this time!" said a voice behind me. "Making Big Ben disappear is a major offense!"

I turned. It was the same policemouse as

before! He was shaking his head and writing **TiCKET** after **TiCKET**.

"Quickly, pull the rope **T** **H** **R** **E** **E** times!" Thea whispered in my ear.

I did. As if by magic, when the curtains opened, Big Ben appeared again!

The audience went wild. *"Bravo! Bravo!"* they shouted.

At that moment, I felt a tap on my shoulder. It was the policemouse.

"I don't know how you put it back," he said, shaking his head. "But don't make it DISAPPEAR again. Got it?"

I nodded. Considering I had no idea how I had made it DISAPPEAR in the first place, I was pretty sure it wouldn't happen again!

"Tell us how you made BIG BEN disappear!" a magician in the front row shouted.

"Yeah, what's the secret?" yelled another.

Before I knew it, the whole crowd was shouting. "Tell us! Tell us! Tell us!"

I froze. What could I say? Would everyone find out I was a fake? "Um, w-well, I . . ." I stammered.

Lucky for me, my sister rushed to my aid.

"A **REAL MAGICIAN** doesn't reveal his secrets!" she insisted.

Phew! Did I mention how much I $love$ my sister?!

Still, there was one SECRET that I did want to reveal to the crowd — the mystery behind the talking lion. It was the whole reason I had traveled to London in the first place!

I turned and faced the audience. When I spotted Mystery Mouse in the crowd, I grinned.

"If Mystery Mouse would be so kind as to come onstage," I said. "I'd like to **SHAKE** the paw of one of my best competitors."

Flattered, Mystery Mouse strode up to the front. I noticed he was still **scratching** like a madmouse, and the skunk odor **WAFTING** off his cape was unmistakable.

Pee-yoo!

He extended his paw for me to shake. Finally, I had the last clue I needed. Mystery Mouse's palm was **glowing** green! It was the exact color of the **FLUORESCENT** paint I had used to paint the handle of the giant suitcase!

I had **PROOF**! Mystery Mouse was the crook I was **LOOKING** for!

Hmm . . .

"You're the rat who's behind the lion statue shouting insults in **Trafalgar Square**!" I squeaked.

Mystery Mouse immediately bolted off the stage and dove into the Thames. He pulled himself into a **SPEEDBOAT** and started zipping away! But before fleeing he shouted,

"It's not over. We will meet again!"

Then he took off his mask and threw it in the river . . . revealing that **he** was a **she**! It was the SHADOW! She is an infamouse thief who I unfortunately know all too well. It wasn't the first time we had crossed paths in a **mysterious** adventure.

The Shadow

I'll be back!

THE SHADOW

The Shadow is Sally Ratmousen's cousin. (Sally is the owner of *The Daily Rat* and Geronimo's bitter rival.) The Shadow will do anything to get rich! She is a master of disguise, and New Mouse City's number one thief!

MISSION ACCOMPLISHED!

The crowd carried me through the streets of London shouting, **"Three cheers** for Geronimo Stilton! The great *Geronimo Stilton*!"

When they finally put me down, Thea, Benjamin, and Bugsy Wugsy ran to **HUG** me. Trap, on the other paw, stood aside, scribbling away furiously in his **Magician's Notebook.** Who knew what he was writing!

A moment later, Professor Ratting appeared by my side. **"THANK YOU**, Mr. Stilton! You solved the mystery and saved the Queen's ***jewels***!"

"Long live the Queen!" the crowd cheered.

Then the professor pinned me with the **Ratonic Medal of Honor**, the highest honor for us mice!

"**CONGRATULATIONS**, Agent 00G," he whispered. "You did a **fabumouse** job!"

I dabbed my **teary** eyes. I must admit

Congratulations!

You're a hero!

Well done, Uncle!

Uncle G ro

I'm a very sentimental mouse. It had been a truly **magical mission** . . . I couldn't have cracked the case without Trap's involvement in the Ultimate Trick!

And that's how this, um, **VACATION** came to an end.

Until next time, dear readers!

Three cheers for Geronimo Stilton!

Hooray!

THE ULTIMATE TRICK!

by TRAP STILTON

Do you know how Geronimo made Big Ben disappear? (Actually, the trick must be credited to Thea, since she's the one who came up with it in the first place.)

Being the greatest magician in the world, I figured it out all on my own!

HERE'S BIG BEN!

NOW BIG BEN'S GONE!

Be sure to read all my fabumouse adventures!

#1 Lost Treasure of the Emerald Eye

#2 The Curse of the Cheese Pyramid

#3 Cat and Mouse in a Haunted House

#4 I'm Too Fond of My Fur!

#5 Four Mice Deep in the Jungle

#6 Paws Off, Cheddarface!

#7 Red Pizzas for a Blue Count

#8 Attack of the Bandit Cats

#9 A Fabumouse Vacation for Geronimo

#10 All Because of a Cup of Coffee

#11 It's Halloween, You 'Fraidy Mouse!

#12 Merry Christmas, Geronimo!

#13 The Phantom of the Subway

#14 The Temple of the Ruby of Fire

#15 The Mona Mousa Code

#16 A Cheese-Colored Camper

#17 Watch Your Whiskers, Stilton!

#18 Shipwreck on the Pirate Islands

#19 My Name Is Stilton, Geronimo Stilton

#20 Surf's Up, Geronimo!

#21 The Wild, Wild West

#22 The Secret of Cacklefur Castle

A Christmas Tale

#23 Valentine's Day Disaster

#24 Field Trip to Niagara Falls

#25 The Search for Sunken Treasure

#26 The Mummy with No Name

#27 The Christmas Toy Factory

#28 Wedding Crasher

#29 Down and Out Down Under

#30 The Mouse Island Marathon

#31 The Mysterious Cheese Thief

Christmas Catastrophe

#32 Valley of the Giant Skeletons

#33 Geronimo and the Gold Medal Mystery

#34 Geronimo Stilton, Secret Agent

#35 A Very Merry Christmas

#36 Geronimo's Valentine

#37 The Race Across America

#38 A Fabumouse School Adventure

#39 Singing Sensation

#40 The Karate Mouse

#41 Mighty Mount Kilimanjaro

#42 The Peculiar Pumpkin Thief

#43 I'm Not a Supermouse!

#44 The Giant Diamond Robbery

#45 Save the White Whale!

#46 The Haunted Castle

#47 Run for the Hills, Geronimo!

#48 The Mystery in Venice

#49 The Way of the Samurai

#50 This Hotel Is Haunted!

#51 The Enormouse Pearl Heist

#52 Mouse in Space!

#53 Rumble in the Jungle

#54 Get into Gear, Stilton!

#55 The Golden Statue Plot

#56 Flight of the Red Bandit

The Hunt for the Golden Book

#57 The Stinky Cheese Vacation

#58 The Super Chef Contest

#59 Welcome to Moldy Manor

The Hunt for the Curious Cheese

#60 The Treasure of Easter Island

#61 Mouse House Hunter

#62 Mouse Overboard!

The Hunt for the Secret Papyrus

#63 The Cheese Experiment

#64 Magical Mission

Up Next:

#65 Bollywood Burglary

MEET
Geronimo Stiltonord

He is a mouseking — the Geronimo Stilton of the ancient far north! He lives with his brawny and brave clan in the village of Mouseborg. From sailing frozen waters to facing fiery dragons, every day is an adventure for the micekings!

#1 Attack of the Dragons

#2 The Famouse Fjord Race

#3 Pull the Dragon's Tooth!

#4 Stay Strong, Geronimo!

Don't miss any of these exciting Thea Sisters adventures!

Thea Stilton and the Dragon's Code

Thea Stilton and the Mountain of Fire

Thea Stilton and the Ghost of the Shipwreck

Thea Stilton and the Secret City

Thea Stilton and the Mystery in Paris

Thea Stilton and the Cherry Blossom Adventure

Thea Stilton and the Star Castaways

Thea Stilton: Big Trouble in the Big Apple

Thea Stilton and the Ice Treasure

Thea Stilton and the Secret of the Old Castle

Thea Stilton and the Blue Scarab Hunt

Thea Stilton and the Prince's Emerald

Thea Stilton and the Mystery on the Orient Express

Thea Stilton and the Dancing Shadows

Thea Stilton and the Legend of the Fire Flowers

Thea Stilton and the Spanish Dance Mission

Thea Stilton and the Journey to the Lion's Den

Thea Stilton and the Great Tulip Heist

Thea Stilton and the Chocolate Sabotage

Thea Stilton and the Missing Myth

Thea Stilton and the Lost Letters

Thea Stilton and the Tropical Treasure

Thea Stilton and the Hollywood Hoax

Thea Stilton and the Madagascar Madness

Don't miss any of my special edition adventures!

THE KINGDOM OF FANTASY

THE QUEST FOR PARADISE:
THE RETURN TO THE KINGDOM OF FANTASY

THE AMAZING VOYAGE:
THE THIRD ADVENTURE IN THE KINGDOM OF FANTASY

THE DRAGON PROPHECY:
THE FOURTH ADVENTURE IN THE KINGDOM OF FANTASY

THE VOLCANO OF FIRE:
THE FIFTH ADVENTURE IN THE KINGDOM OF FANTASY

THE SEARCH FOR TREASURE:
THE SIXTH ADVENTURE IN THE KINGDOM OF FANTASY

THE ENCHANTED CHARMS:
THE SEVENTH ADVENTURE IN THE KINGDOM OF FANTASY

THE PHOENIX OF DESTINY:
AN EPIC KINGDOM OF FANTASY ADVENTURE

THE HOUR OF MAGIC:
THE EIGHTH ADVENTURE IN THE KINGDOM OF FANTASY

THE WIZARD'S WAND:
THE NINTH ADVENTURE IN THE KINGDOM OF FANTASY

THE JOURNEY THROUGH TIME

BACK IN TIME:
THE SECOND JOURNEY THROUGH TIME

THE RACE AGAINST TIME:
THE THIRD JOURNEY THROUGH TIME

LOST IN TIME:
THE FOURTH JOURNEY THROUGH TIME

MEET
GERONIMO STILTONIX

He is a spacemouse — the Geronimo Stilton of a parallel universe! He is captain of the spaceship *MouseStar 1*. While flying through the cosmos, he visits distant planets and meets crazy aliens. His adventures are out of this world!

#1 Alien Escape

#2 You're Mine, Captain!

#3 Ice Planet Adventure

#4 The Galactic Goal

#5 Rescue Rebellion

#6 The Underwater Planet

#7 Beware! Space Junk!

#8 Away in a Star Sled

#9 Slurp Monster Showdown

Meet
GERONIMO STILTONOOT

He is a cavemouse—Geronimo Stilton's ancient ancestor! He runs the stone newspaper in the prehistoric village of Old Mouse City. From dealing with dinosaurs to dodging meteorites, his life in the Stone Age is full of adventure!

#1 The Stone of Fire

#2 Watch Your Tail!

#3 Help, I'm in Hot Lava!

#4 The Fast and the Frozen

#5 The Great Mouse Race

#6 Don't Wake the Dinosaur!

#7 I'm a Scaredy-Mouse!

#8 Surfing for Secrets

#9 Get the Scoop, Geronimo!

#10 My Autosaurus Will Win!

#11 Sea Monster Surprise

#12 Paws Off the Pearl!

#13 The Smelly Search

ABOUT THE AUTHOR

 Born in New Mouse City, Mouse Island, **GERONIMO STILTON** is Rattus Emeritus of Mousomorphic Literature and of Neo-Ratonic Comparative Philosophy. For the past twenty years, he has been running *The Rodent's Gazette*, New Mouse City's most widely read daily newspaper.

Stilton was awarded the Ratitzer Prize for his scoops on *The Curse of the Cheese Pyramid* and *The Search for Sunken Treasure*. He has also received the Andersen 2000 Prize for Personality of the Year. One of his bestsellers won the 2002 eBook Award for world's best ratlings' electronic book. His works have been published all over the globe.

In his spare time, Mr. Stilton collects antique cheese rinds and plays golf. But what he most enjoys is telling stories to his nephew Benjamin.

1. Main entrance
2. Printing presses (where the books and newspaper are printed)
3. Accounts department
4. Editorial room (where the editors, illustrators, and designers work)
5. Geronimo Stilton's office
6. Helicopter landing pad

THE RODENT'S GAZETTE

Map of New Mouse City

Map of Mouse Island

Dear mouse friends,
Thanks for reading, and farewell
till the next book.
It'll be another whisker-licking-good
adventure, and that's a promise!

Geronimo Stilton